Right Place, Right Time

Leslie McKelvey

self as clown in a great pantomime, to be knocked down, and pulled up, slashed, tickled, and buttered *à discrétion* for the benefit of a manual-pleasantry-loving Public. So it would be weakness in him to complain of bruised back, scored elbows, and bumped head.

Besides, the treatment you receive varies prodigiously according to the temper and the manifold influences from without that operate upon the gentleman that operates upon you. For instance—

" 'Tis a *failure* at being *funny*," says surly Aristarchus, when, for some reason or other, he dislikes you or your publisher.

" It is a *smart* book," opines another, who has no particular reason to be your friend.

" Narrated with *freshness of thought*," declares a third, who takes an honest pride in "giving the devil his due."

" Very *clever*," exclaims the amiable critic, who for some reason or another likes you or your publisher.

"There is *wit* and *humour* in these pages," says the gentleman who has some particular reason to be your friend.

" Evinces considerable *talent*."

And—

" There is *genius* in this book," declare the dear critics who in any way identify themselves or their interests with you.

Now for the extract :—

" Mr. Burton was, it appears, stationed for several years in Sind with his regiment, and it is due to him to say that he has set a good example to his fellow-subalterns by pursuing so diligently his inquiries into the language, literature, and customs of the native population by which he was surrounded. We are far from accepting all his doctrines on questions of Eastern policy, especially as regards the treatment of natives; but we are sensible of the value of the additional evidence which he has brought forward on many important questions. For a young man, he seems to have adopted some very extreme opinions; and it is perhaps not too much to say, that the fault from which he has most to fear, not only as an author, but as an Indian officer, is a disregard of those well-established rules of moderation which no one can transgress with impunity."

The greatest difficulty a raw writer on Indian subjects has to contend with is a proper comprehension of the *ignorance crasse* which besets the mind of the home-reader and his oracle the critic. What a knowledge these lines do show of the opportunity for study presented to the Anglo-Indian subaltern serving with his corps! Part of the time when I did duty with mine we were quartered at Ghárrá, a heap of bungalows surrounded by a wall of milk-bush; on a sandy flat, near a dirty village whose timorous inhabitants shunned us as walking pestilences. No amount of domiciliary visitings would have found a single Sindian book in the place, except the accounts of the native shopkeepers; and, to the best of my remembrance, there was not a soul who could make himself intelligible in the common medium of Indian intercourse—Hindostani. An ensign stationed at Dover Castle might write "Ellis's Antiquities;" a *sous-lieutenant* with his corps at Boulogne might compose the "Legendaire de la Morinie," but Ghárrá was sufficient to paralyse the readiest pen that ever coursed over foolscap paper.

Now, waiving, with all due modesty, the unmerited compliment of "good boy," so gracefully tendered to me, I proceed to the judgment which follows it, my imminent peril of "extreme opinions." If there be any value in the "additional evidence" I have "brought forward on important questions," the reader may, perchance, be curious to know how that evidence was collected. So, without further apology, I plunge into the subject.

After some years of careful training for the Church in the north and south of France, Florence, Naples, and the University of Pisa, I found myself one day walking the High Street, Oxford, with all the emotions which a Parisian exquisite of the first water would experience on awaking—at 3 P.M.,—in "Dandakaran's tangled wood."

To be brief, my "college career" was highly unsatisfactory. I began a "reading man," worked regularly twelve hours a day, failed in everything—chiefly, I flattered myself, because Latin hexameters and Greek iambics had not entered into the list of my studies—threw up the classics, and returned to old habits of fencing, boxing, and single-stick, handling the "ribbons," and sketching facetiously, though not wisely, the reverend features and figures of certain half-reformed monks, calling themselves "fellows." My reading also ran into bad courses—Erpenius, Zadkiel, Falconry, Cornelius, Agrippa, and the Art of Pluck.

At last the Afghan war broke out. After begging the paternal authority in vain for the Austrian service, the Swiss Guards at Naples, and even the *Légion étrangère*, I determined to leave Oxford, *coûte qui coûte*. The testy old lady, Alma Mater, was easily persuaded to consign, for a time, to "country nursing" the froward brat who showed not a whit of filial regard for her. So, after two years, I left Trinity, without a "little go," in a high dog-cart,—a companion in misfortune too-tooing lustily through a "yard of tin," as the dons started up from their game of bowls to witness the departure of the forbidden vehicle. Thus having thoroughly established the fact that I was fit for nothing but to be "shot at for sixpence a day," and as those Afghans (how I blessed their name!) had cut gaps in many a regiment, my father provided me with a commission in the Indian army, and started me as quickly as feasible for the "land of the sun."

So, my friends and fellow-soldiers, I may address you in the words of the witty thief—slightly altered from Gil Blas—"Blessings on the dainty pow of the old dame who turned me out of her house; for had she shown clemency I should now doubtless be a dyspeptic Don, instead of which I have the honour to be a lieutenant, your comrade."

As the Bombay pilot sprang on board, twenty mouths agape over the gangway, all asked one and the same question. Alas! the answer was a sad one!—the Afghans had been defeated—the avenging army had retreated! The twenty mouths all ejaculated a something unfit for ears polite.

To a mind thoroughly impressed with the sentiment that

"Man wants but little here below,
Nor wants that little long,"

the position of an ensign in the Hon. E. I. Company's Service is a very satisfactory one. He has a horse or two, part of a house, a pleasant mess, plenty of pale ale, as much shooting as he can manage, and an occasional invitation to a dance, where there are thirty-two cavaliers to three dames, or to a dinner-party when a chair unexpectedly falls vacant. But some are vain enough to want more, and of these fools was I.

In India two roads lead to preferment. **The** direct highway is "service ;"—getting a flesh **wound**, cutting down a few of the **enemy, and doing something** eccentric, so that your **name may** creep into **a despatch.** The other path, **study of** the languages, **is a** rugged and tortuous one, **still** you have only to plod **steadily** along its length, **and,** sooner **or later,** you must come **to a** " staff appointment." *Bien entendu,* I suppose you **to be** destitute **of or** deficient in interest whose magic influence **sets** you down at once a heaven-born Staff Officer, **at the** goal which others must toil to reach.

A dozen lessons from Professor Forbes and **a native** servant on board the *John Knox* enabled me to land with *éclat* as a griff, and to astonish the throng of palanquin bearers that jostled, pushed, **and** pulled **me at the** pier head, **with the** vivacity **and** nervousness **of my** phraseology. **And I spent the** first evening in **company** with one **Dossabhoee Sorabjee, a white-bearded Parsee,** who, in his quality of **language-master, had** vernacularized the tongues of Hormuzd knows how many generations of Anglo-Indian subalterns.

The **corps to** which I was appointed was then in country quarters at Baroda, in the land of Guzerat; the journey was a long one, the difficulty of finding good instructors there was **great, so was the** expense, moreover fevers abounded ; **and, lastly,** it was not so **easy to** obtain leave of absence **to visit the** Presidency, **where** candidates **for the** honours of language are examined. These were serious obstacles to success ; they were surmounted, **however, in** six months, at the end of which time I found **myself in the** novel position of "passed interpreter in Hindostani."

My success—for I had distanced a field of eleven— **encouraged me to a** second attempt, and though I had to front all the difficulties over again, in four months my name appeared in orders as qualified to interpret in the Guzerattee tongue.

Meanwhile the Ameers of Sind had exchanged their palaces at Haydarábád for other quarters not quite so comfortable at Hazareebagh, and we were ordered up to the Indus for the pleasant purpose of acting police there. Knowing the Conqueror's chief want, a man who could speak a word of his pet conquests' vernacular dialect, I had not been a week at Karáchee before I found a language-master and a book. But the study was undertaken *invitâ minervâ.* We were quartered in tents, duststorms howled over us daily, drills and brigade parades were never ending, and, as I was acting interpreter to my regiment, courts-martial of dreary length occupied the best part of my time. Besides, it was impossible to work in such an atmosphere of discontent. The seniors abhorred the barren desolate spot, with all its inglorious perils of fever, spleen, dysentery, and congestion of the brain, the juniors grumbled in sympathy, and the Staff officers, ordered up to rejoin the corps—it was on field service—complained bitterly of having to quit their comfortable appointments in more favoured lands without even a campaign in prospect. So when, a month or two after landing in the country, we were transferred from Karáchee to Ghárrá—purgatory to the other locale—I threw aside Sindí for Maharatte, hoping, by dint of reiterated examinations, to escape the place of torment as soon as possible. It was very like studying Russian in an English country-town; however, with the assistance of Molesworth's excellent dictionary, and the regimental Pundit, or schoolmaster, I gained some knowledge of the dialect, and proved myself duly qualified in it at Bombay. At the same time a brother subaltern and I had jointly leased a Persian Moonshee, one Mirza Mohammed Hosayn, of Shiraz. Poor fellow, after passing through the fires of Sind unscathed, he returned to his delightful land for a few weeks, to die there!—and we laid the foundation of a lengthened course of reading in that most elegant of Oriental languages.

Now it is a known fact that a good Staff appointment has the general effect of doing away with one's bad opinion of any place whatever. So when, by the kindness of a friend whose name *his* modesty prevents my mentioning, the Governor of Sind was persuaded to give me the temporary appointment of Assistant in the Survey, I began to look with interest upon the desolation around me. The country was a new one, so was its population, so was their language. After reading all the works published upon the subject, I felt convinced that none but Mr. Crow and Capt. J. McMurdo had dipped beneath the superficies of things. My new duties compelled me to spend the cold season in wandering over the districts, levelling the beds of canals, and making preparatory sketches for a grand survey. I was thrown so entirely amongst the people as to depend upon them for society, and the "dignity," not to mention the increased allowances of a Staff officer, enabled me to collect a fair stock of books, and to gather around me those who could make them of any use. So, after the first year, when I had Persian at my fingers' ends, sufficient Arabic to read, write, and converse fluently, and a superficial knowledge of that dialect of Punjaubee which is spoken in the wilder parts of the province, I began the systematic study of the Sindian people, their manners and their tongue.

The first difficulty was to pass for an Oriental, and this was as necessary as it was difficult. The European

official in India seldom, if ever, sees anything in its real
light, so dense is the veil which the fearfulness, the
duplicity, the prejudice, and the superstitions of the
natives hang before his eyes. And the white man lives
a life so distinct from the black, that hundreds of the
former serve through what they call their "term of
exile" without once being present at a circumcision feast,
a wedding, or a funeral. More especially the present
generation, whom the habit and the means of taking fur-
loughs, the increased facility for enjoying ladies' society,
and, if truth be spoken, a greater regard for appearances,
if not a stricter code of morality, estrange from their
dusky fellow-subjects every day and day the more.
After trying several characters, the easiest to be assumed
was, I found, that of a half Arab, half Iranian, such as
may be met with in thousands along the northern shore
of the Persian Gulf. The Sindians would have detected
in a moment the difference between my articulation and
their own, had I attempted to speak their vernacular
dialect, but they attributed the accent to my strange
country, as naturally as a home-bred Englishman would
account for the bad pronunciation of a foreigner calling
himself partly Spanish, partly Portuguese. Besides, I
knew the countries along the Gulf by heart from books,
I had a fair knowledge of the Shiah form of worship pre-
valent in Persia, and my poor Moonshee was generally at
hand to support me in times of difficulty, so that the
danger of being detected—even by a "real Simon Pure"
—was a very inconsiderable one.

With hair falling upon his shoulders, a long beard,
face and hands, arms and feet, stained with a thin coat
of henna, Mirza Abdullah of Bushire—your humble servant—set out upon many and many a trip. He was a
Bazzaz, a vendor of fine linen, calicoes, and muslins—

such chapmen are sometimes admitted to display their wares, even in the sacred harem, by "fast" and fashionable dames—and he had a little pack of *bijouterie* and *virtù* reserved for emergencies. It was only, however, when absolutely necessary that he displayed his stock-in-trade; generally, he contented himself with alluding to it on all possible occasions, boasting largely of his traffic, and asking a thousand questions concerning the state of the market. Thus he could walk into most men's houses, quite without ceremony; even if the master dreamed of kicking him out, the mistress was sure to oppose such measure with might and main. He secured numberless invitations, was proposed to by several papas, and won, or had to think he won, a few hearts; for he came as a rich man and he stayed with dignity, and he departed exacting all the honours. When wending his ways he usually urged a return of visit in the morning, but he was seldom to be found at the caravanserai he specified—was Mirza Abdullah the Bushiri.

The timid villagers collected in crowds to see the rich merchant in Oriental dress, riding spear in hand, and pistols in holsters, towards the little encampment pitched near their settlements. But regularly every evening on the line of march the Mirza issued from his tent and wandered amongst them, collecting much information and dealing out more concerning an ideal master—the Feringhee supposed to be sitting in State amongst the Moonshees, the Scribes, the servants, the wheels, the chains, the telescopes, and the other magical inplements in which the camp abounded. When travelling, the Mirza became this mysterious person's factotum, and often had he to answer the question how much his perquisites and illicit gains amounted to in the course of the year.

When the Mirza arrived at a strange town, his first step was to secure a house in or near the bazaar, for the purpose of evening *conversazioni*. Now and then he rented a shop, and furnished it with clammy dates, viscid molasses, tobacco, ginger, rancid oil, and strong-smelling sweetmeats; and wonderful tales Fame told about these establishments. Yet somehow or other, though they were more crowded than a first-rate milliner's rooms in town, they throve not in a pecuniary point of view; the cause of which was, I believe, that the polite Mirza was in the habit of giving the heaviest possible weight for their money to all the ladies, particularly the pretty ones, that honoured him by patronizing his concern.

Sometimes the Mirza passed the evening in a mosque listening to the ragged students who, stretched at full length with their stomachs on the dusty floor, and their arms supporting their heads, mumbled out Arabic from the thumbed, soiled, and tattered pages of theology upon which a dim oil light shed its scanty ray, or he sat debating the niceties of faith with the long-bearded, shaven-pated, blear-eyed, and stolid faced *genus loci*, the Mullah. At other times, when in merrier mood, he entered uninvited the first door whence issued the sounds of music and the dance;—a clean turban and a polite bow are the best "tickets for soup" the East knows. Or he played chess with some native friend, or he consorted with the hemp-drinkers and opium-eaters in the *estaminets*, or he visited the Mrs. Gadabouts and Go-betweens who make matches amongst the Faithful, and gathered from them a precious budget of private history and domestic scandal.

What scenes he saw! what adventures he went through! But who would believe, even if he ventured to detail them?

The Mirza's favourite school for study was the house
of an elderly matron on the banks of the Fulailee
River, about a mile from the Fort of Haydarábád.
Khanum Jan had been a beauty in her youth, and the
tender passion had been hard upon her—at least judging
from the fact that she had fled her home, her husband,
and her native town, Candahar, in company with
Mohammed Bakhsh, a purblind old tailor, the object of
her warmest affections.

"Ah, he is a regular old hyæna now," would the Joan
exclaim in her outlandish Persian, pointing to the vener-
able Darby as he sat in the cool shade, nodding his
head and winking his eyes over a pair of pantaloons
which took him a month to sew, "but you should have
seen him fifteen years ago, what a wonderful youth he
was!"

The knowledge of one mind is that of a million—after
a fashion. I. addressed myself particularly to that of
"Darby;" and many an hour of tough thought it took
me before I had mastered its truly Oriental peculiarities,
its regular irregularities of deduction, and its strange
monotonous one-idea'dness.

Khanum Jan's house was a mud edifice, occupying one
side of a square formed by tall, thin, crumbling mud
walls. The respectable matron's peculiar vanity was to
lend a helping hand in all manner of *affaires du cœur*. So
it often happened that Mirza Abdullah was turned out of
the house to pass a few hours in the garden. There he
sat upon his felt rug spread beneath a shadowy tama-
rind, with beds of sweet-smelling basil around him, his
eyes roving over the broad river that coursed rapidly
between its wooded banks and the groups gathered at
the frequent ferries, whilst the soft strains of mysterious,
philosophical, transcendental Hafiz were sounded in his

ears by the other Meerza, his companion, Mohammed Hosayn—peace be upon him!

Of all economical studies this course was the cheapest. For tobacco daily, for frequent draughts of milk, for hemp occasionally, for the benefit of Khanum Jan's experience, for four months' lectures from Mohammed Bakhsh, and for sundry other little indulgences, the Mirza paid, it is calculated, the sum of six shillings. When he left Haydarábád, he gave a silver talisman to the dame, and a cloth coat to her protector : long may they live to wear them !

  *   *   *   *   *

Thus it was I formed my estimate of the native character. I am as ready to reform it when a man of more extensive experience and greater knowledge of the subject will kindly show me how far it transgresses the well-established limits of moderation. As yet I hold, by way of general rule, that the Eastern mind—I talk of the nations known to me by personal experience—is always in extremes ; that it ignores what is meant by "golden mean," and that it delights to range in flights limited only by the *ne plus ultra* of Nature herself. Under which conviction I am open to correction.

RICHARD F. BURTON.